dancing bear

Manasi Subramaniam
Gwangjo, Jung–a Park

On the morning of Altaf's twelfth birthday, he found Somu tied to the gulmohar tree outside his house.

'That's your birthday gift!' Altaf's father called out from inside.

Altaf could hardly contain his joy. Somu was no ordinary gift! He was a sloth bear with big, furry arms, beautiful brown eyes and a silver v-shaped mark on his chest that made him look magical.

Altaf's father smiled as he stepped out. 'You're a big boy now, Altaf,' he said, 'Train Somu well. Take him to the streets everyday. The more you earn, the prouder I will be.'

Altaf nodded earnestly. This was the best birthday gift he could have asked for!

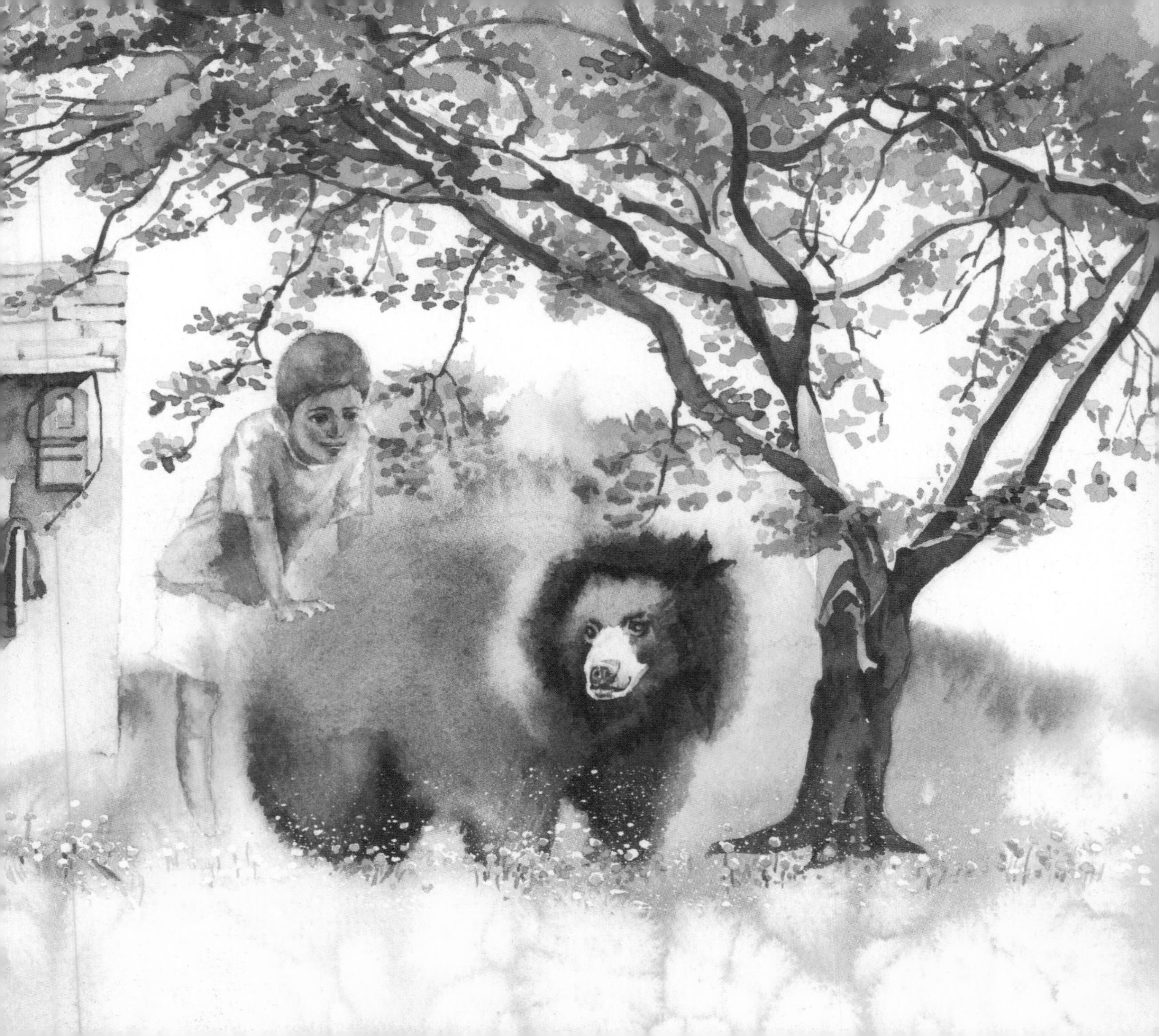

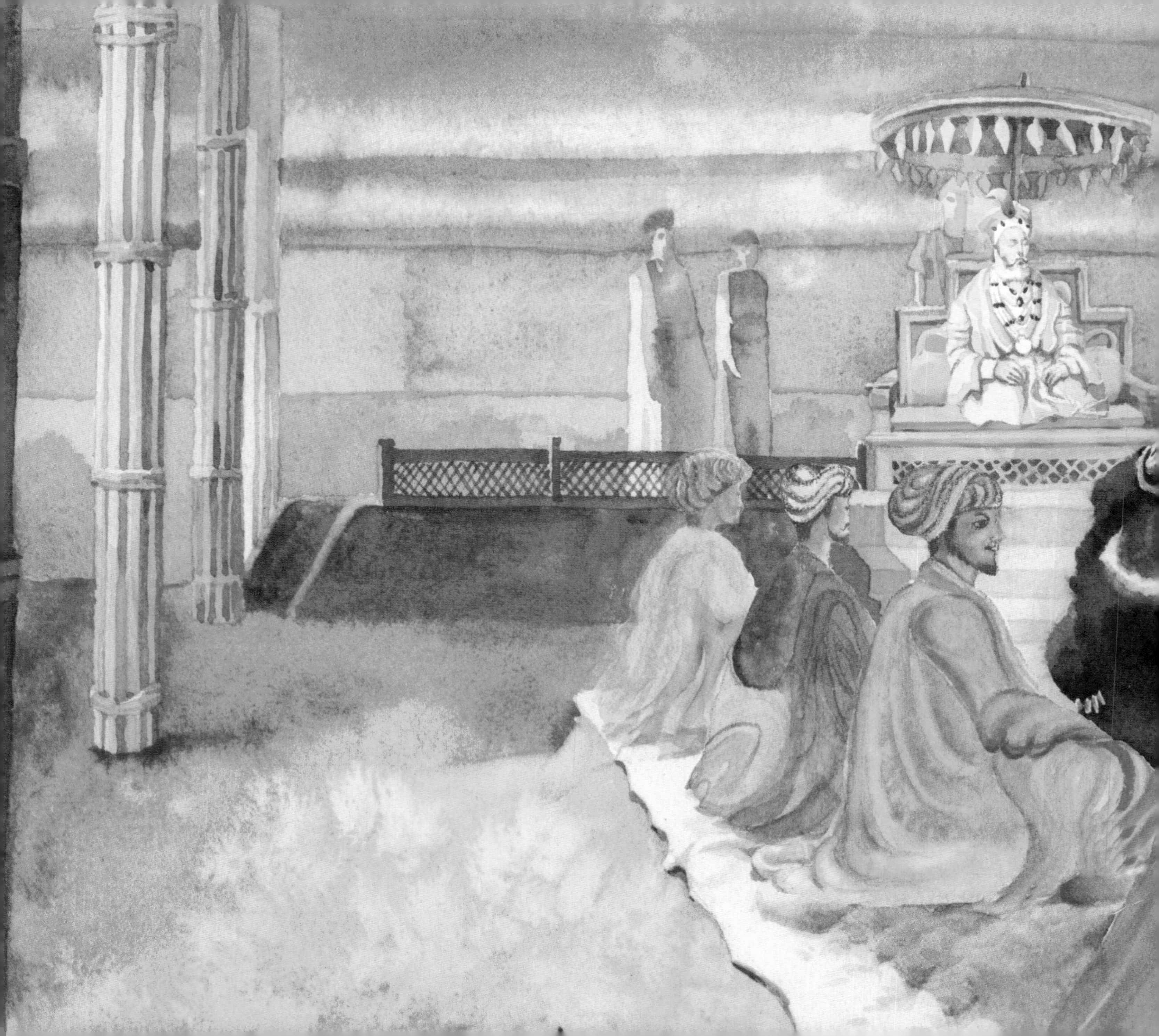

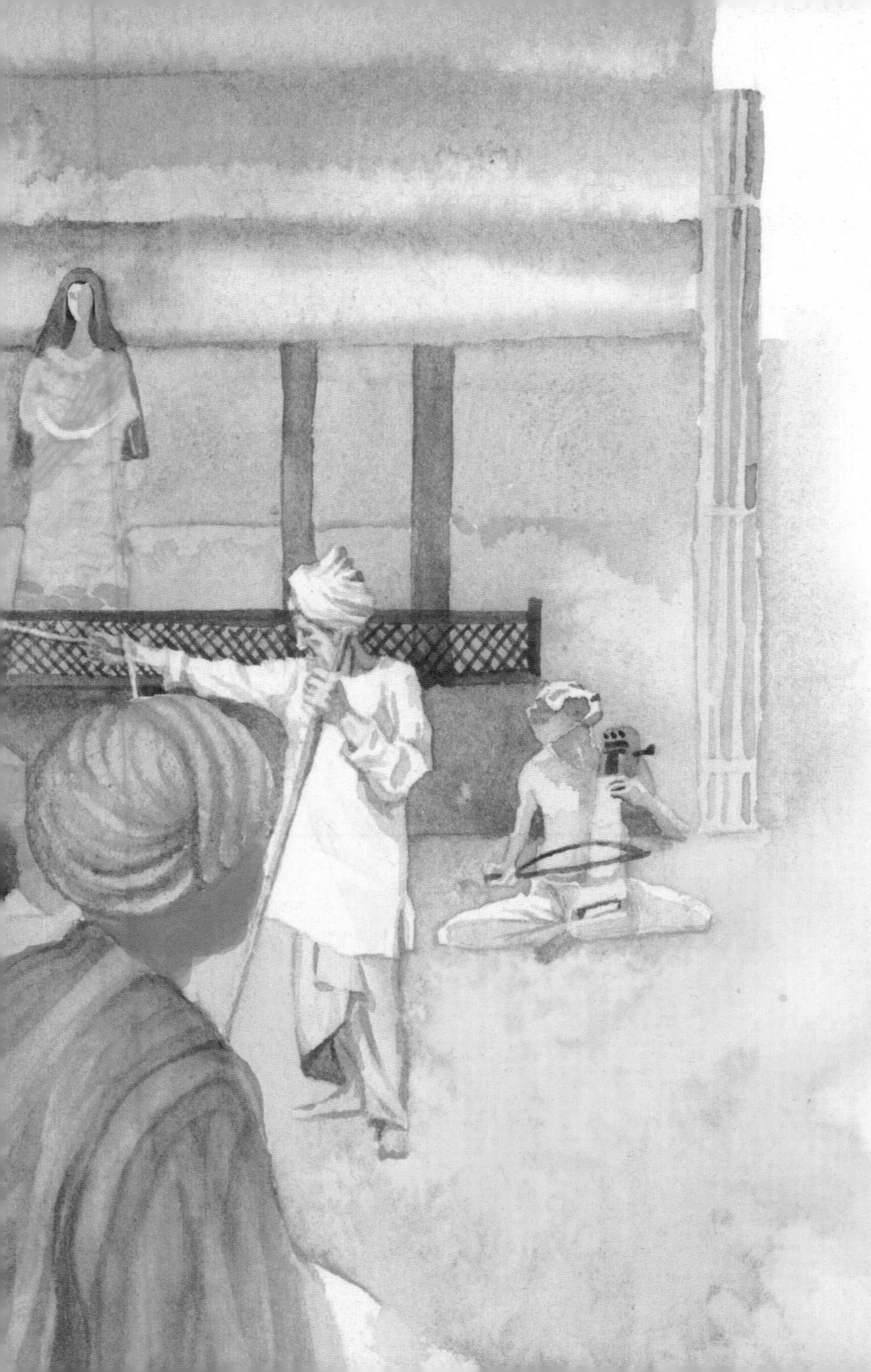

For generations, Altaf's family had been working with dancing bears. They were the Qalandars, an ancient gypsy tribe descended from the royal entertainers of the Mughal emperors.

It was a profession that had been handed down from generation to generation.

Altaf was proud of his great ancestry, and he couldn't wait to go dancing with Somu!

Early the next morning, Altaf got to work.
He went to the gulmohur tree and gently
untied Somu.

'Shall we dance?' he murmured softly.

In a low voice, Altaf began to hum.
Somu pricked up his ears and rose slowly.
He raised his arms and twirled.

As Altaf's song gained momentum,
Somu pranced gracefully from side to side.

Altaf began to clap. Things were going
well indeed!

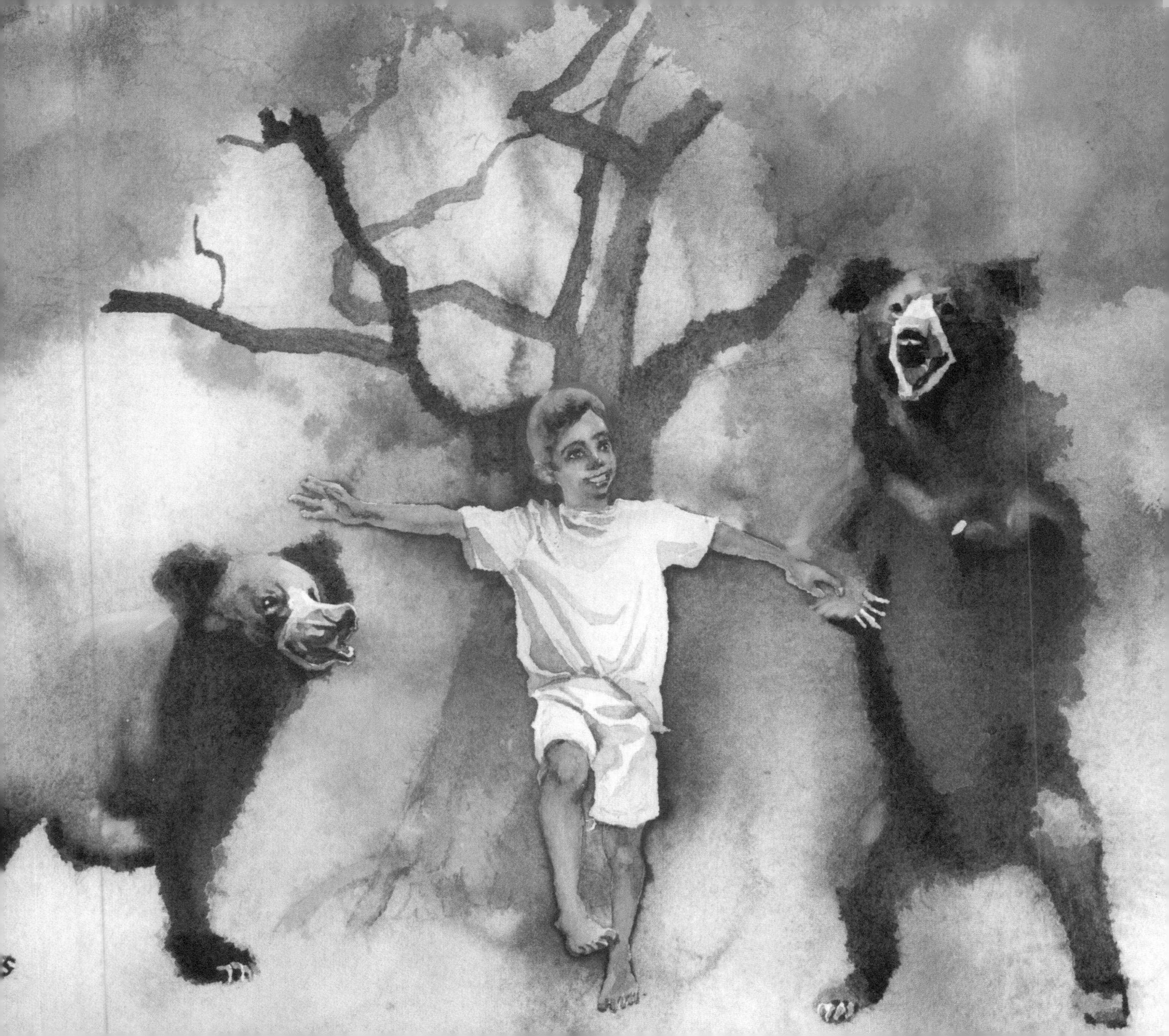

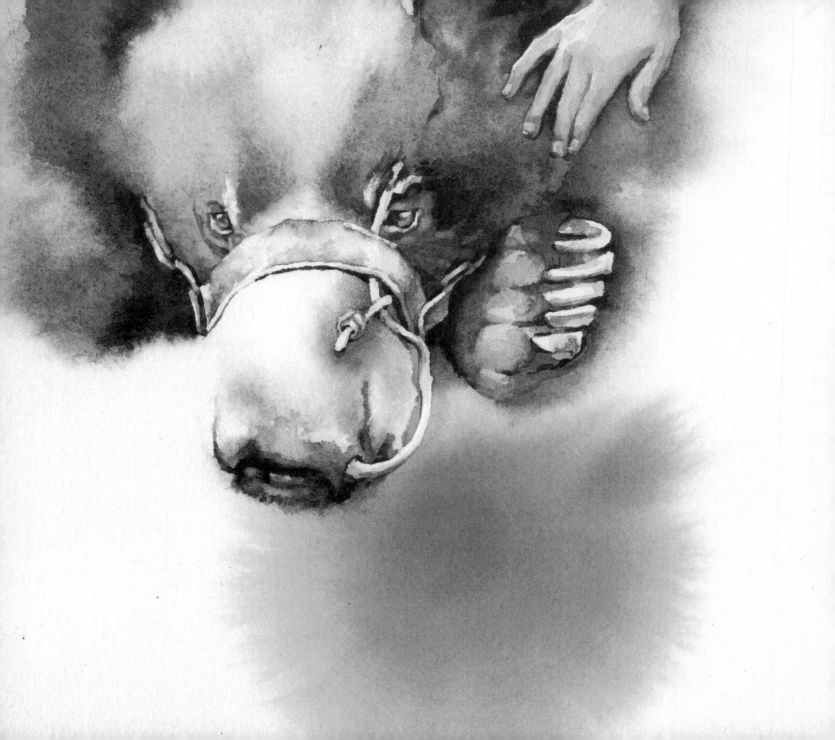

Altaf held out a handful of nuts to Somu as a reward. When Somu leaned forward to nibble on them, Altaf noticed his heavy breathing and panting. Somu looked exhausted.

'What's the matter, Somu? Are you falling sick?' asked Altaf, concernedly stroking the big bear between his ears. As his hands travelled across Somu's head, Altaf felt something damp and sticky.

Altaf gasped. Somu was bleeding at the mouth!

Right where the rope was inserted through Somu's muzzle, there were several cuts in Somu's jaw and a steady flow of blood.

Worriedly, Altaf tied Somu to the gulmohar tree once more and ran inside to find his father.

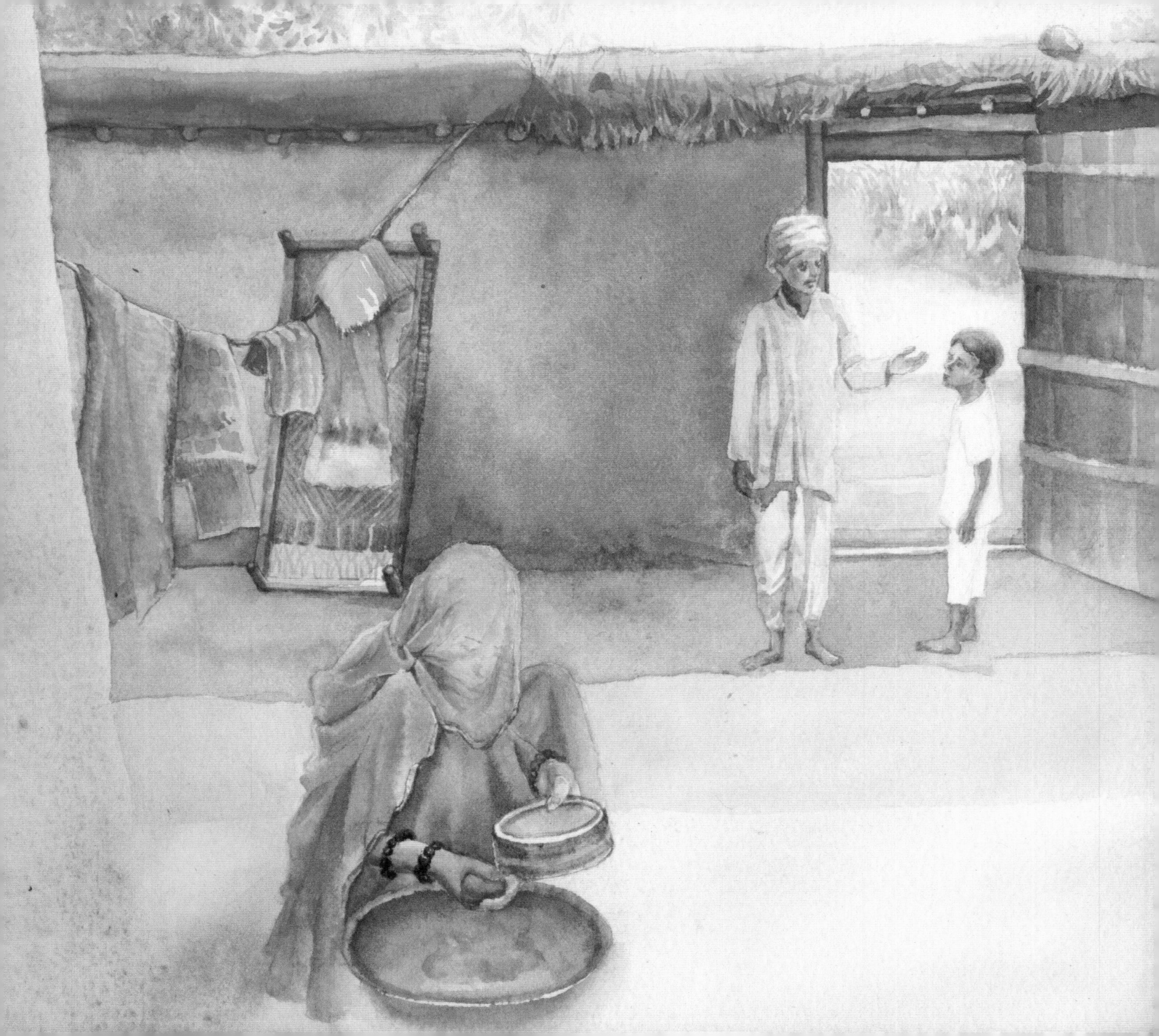

‘Papa, Somu is bleeding!’ Altaf cried.

Altaf’s father caught him by the shoulders. ‘Calm down, Altaf! These things happen. The bleeding will stop on its own.’

‘But Papa!’ exclaimed Altaf, ‘How did that rope get through Somu’s mouth?’

‘We inserted it when he was a little cub. I am sure Somu is used to it by now.’

Altaf was horrified. ‘How, Papa? How did you make a hole in Somu’s muzzle?’

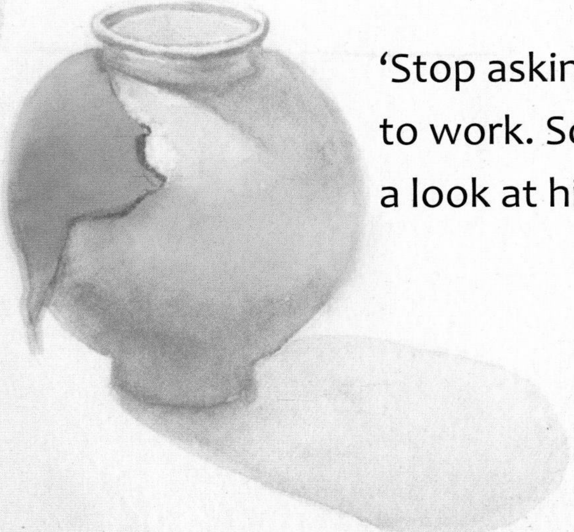

‘Stop asking all these questions and get back to work. Somu will be fine. I will come and take a look at him later,’ said his father impatiently.

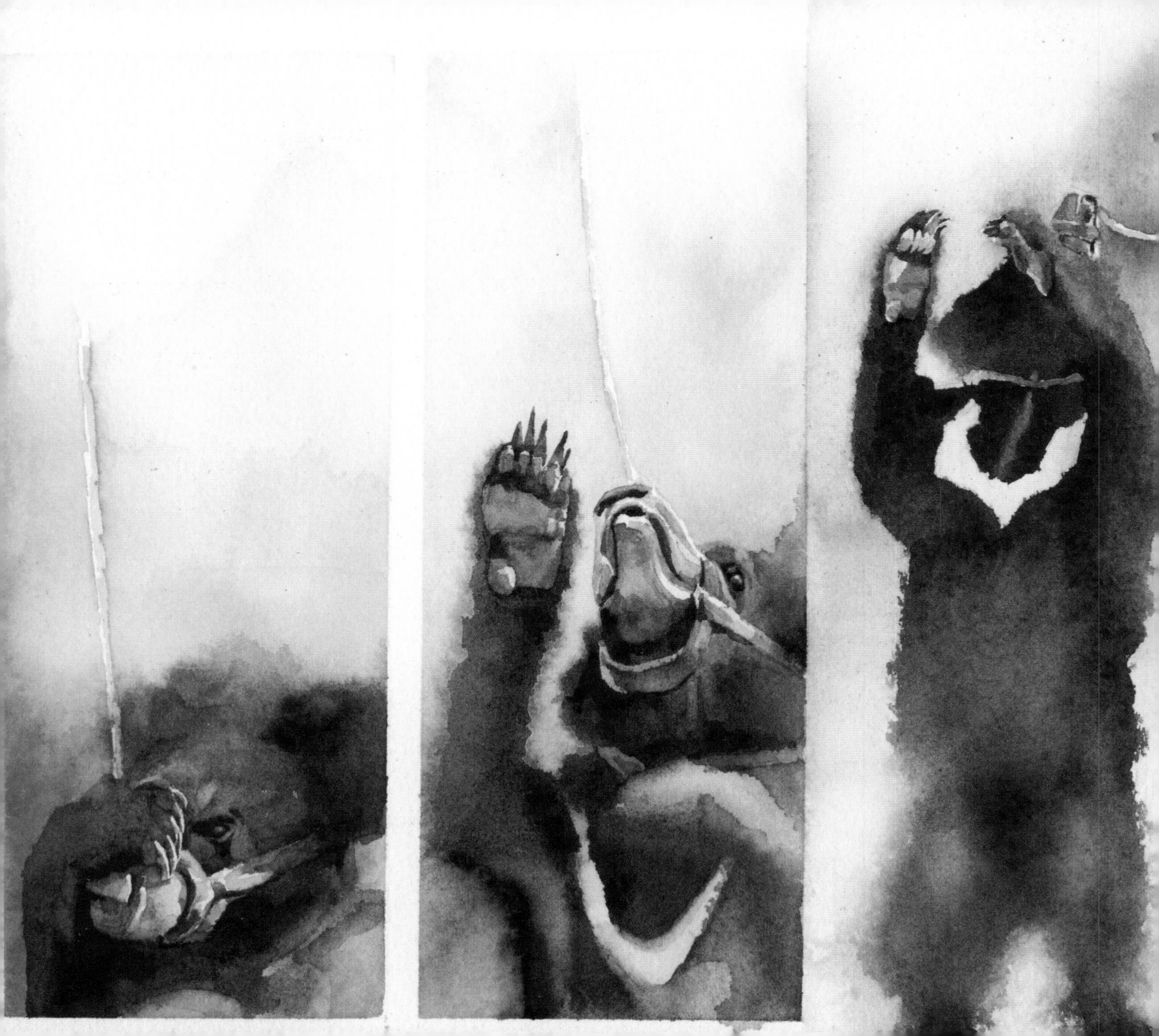

Confused and disturbed, Altaf returned to the gulmohar tree and held his hand out for Somu to step up. But Somu didn't.

'Come on, Somu,' Altaf cajoled, 'How will we practice?'

Suddenly, he heard a voice behind him. 'He won't come if you ask so nicely.'

It was Bavik Chacha. Behind him stood Toufan, his bear, led by a rope. As if to prove his point, Bavik Chacha pulled hard at the rope. With a squeal of pain, Toufan stepped up.

Altaf's eyes were wide with astonishment. Why was Bavik Chacha so cruel to Toufan? After all, Toufan was the best dancer among the bears.

Bavik Chacha then dragged Toufan out into the courtyard and ordered him to dance. With a whip, he lashed out hard on Toufan's back.

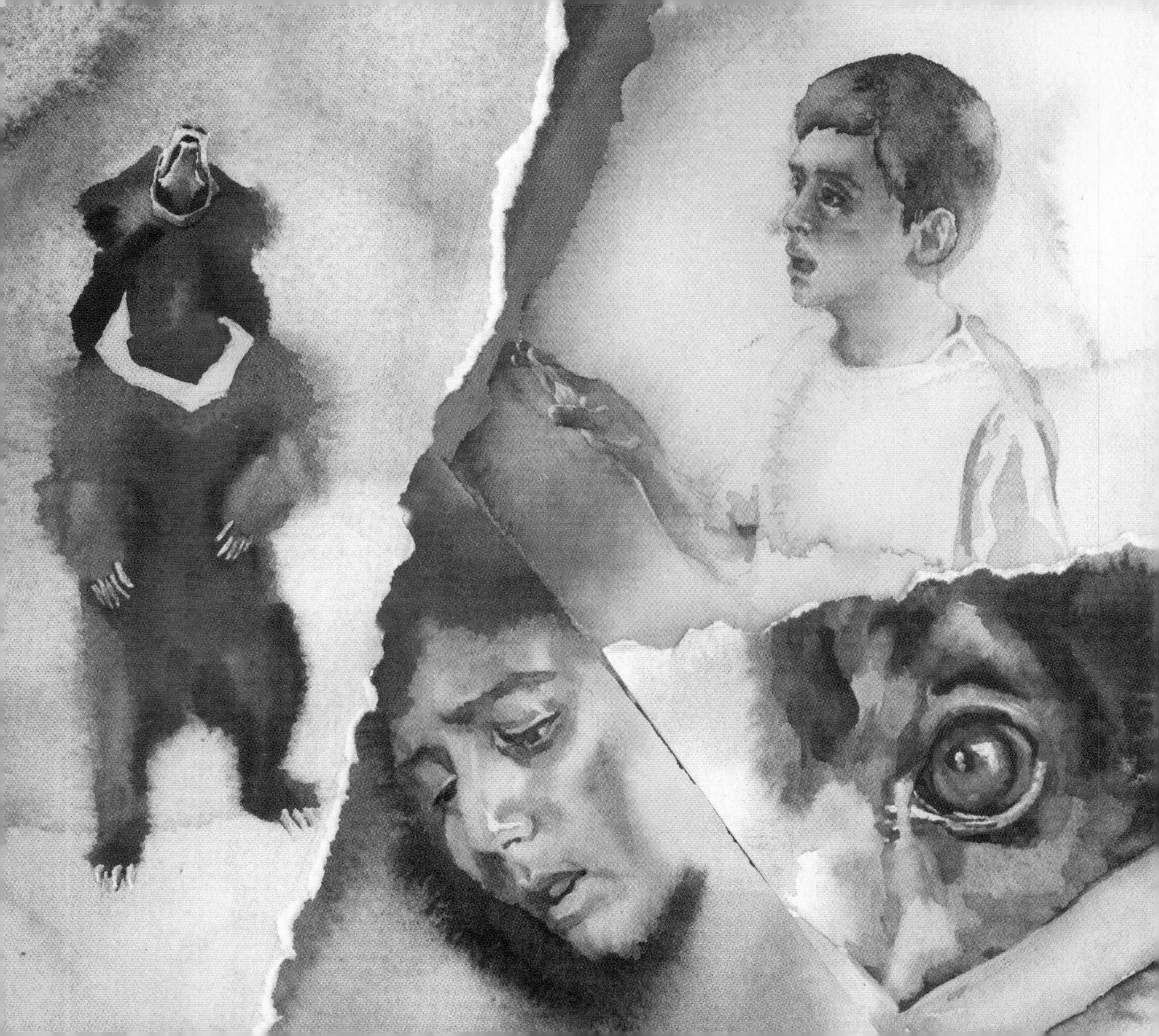

Altaf was horrified. He looked pleadingly at Somu and said once more, 'Come on, Somu.'

But Somu, still tired and bleeding, refused.

Bavik Chacha was watching him from the courtyard and Altaf didn't want to look foolish in front of the great man. He nervously grabbed Somu's rope and tugged hard. Somu squealed with pain, but allowed himself to be pulled up.

With an air of forced bravado, Altaf dragged Somu along and headed to the marketplace.

But at the pit of his stomach was a nasty feeling that simply wouldn't go away.

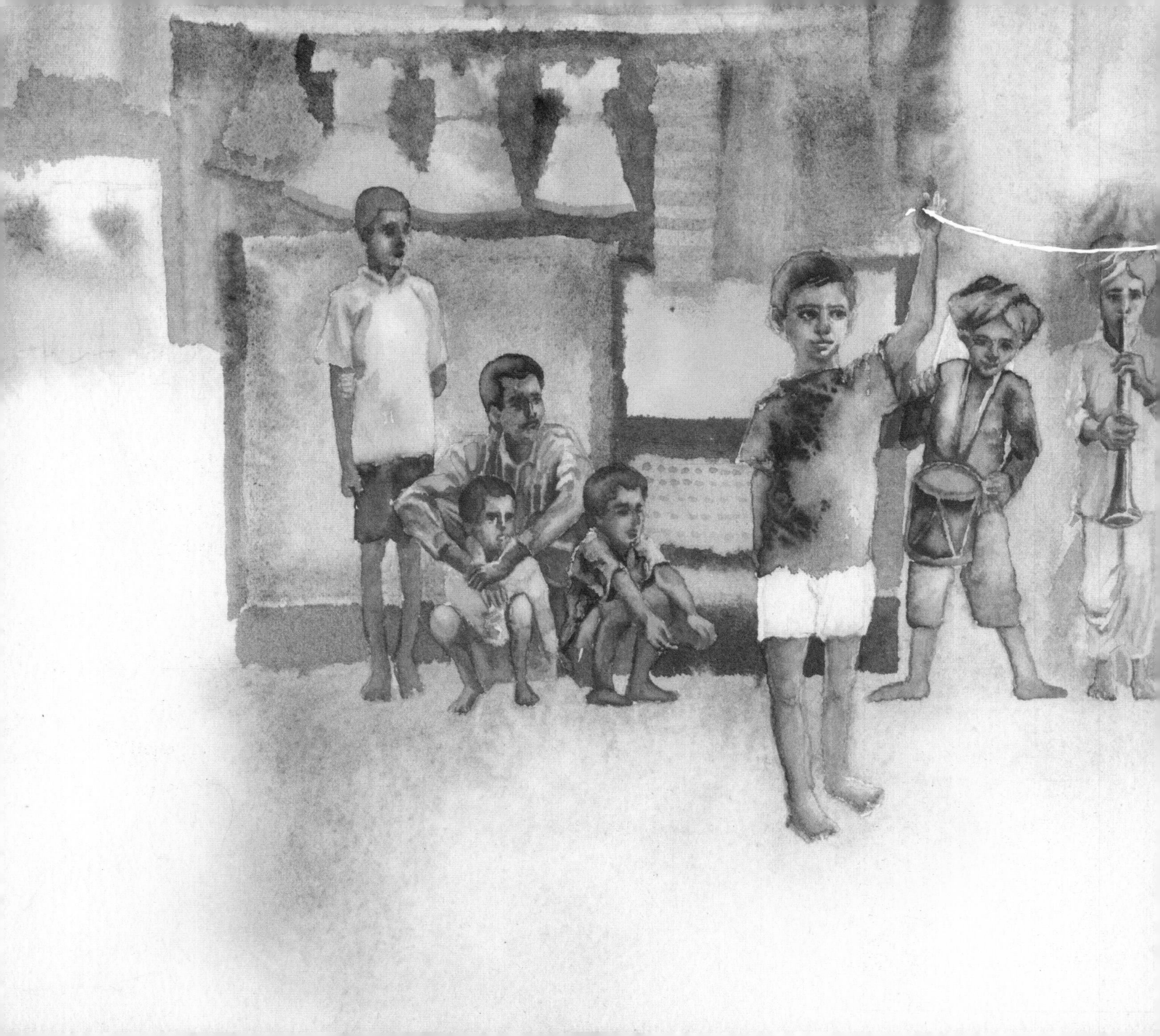

At the marketplace, Altaf held Somu's rope tight and pulled him into a dance.

Soon, a crowd began to gather. Somu danced and danced, and every time he seemed tired, Altaf instinctively pulled at the rope to make him continue.

At the end of the dance, everyone clapped and cheered and flung coins at Somu, who took a few last steps and slumped to the ground.

Excited that their first dance had gone so well, Altaf was about to start another one. But as he tugged, Somu, instead of stepping up, just looked away and stayed settled on the dusty ground.

Altaf didn't know what to do. Feeling miserable, he sat down next to Somu. 'What's the matter, old friend? Don't you like dancing anymore?' But Somu didn't even look up.

After what seemed like hours, Somu rose slowly and allowed Altaf to lead him back home. The feeling at the pit of his stomach grew stronger and nastier. Ignoring it, Altaf chattered away.

'You're just tired, today, aren't you Somu? Don't worry. Rest today. We'll start again tomorrow. We'll become a more famous team than Bavik Chacha and Toufan.'

But no matter how cheerily he talked, Somu didn't respond. Altaf felt like he had lost his best friend.

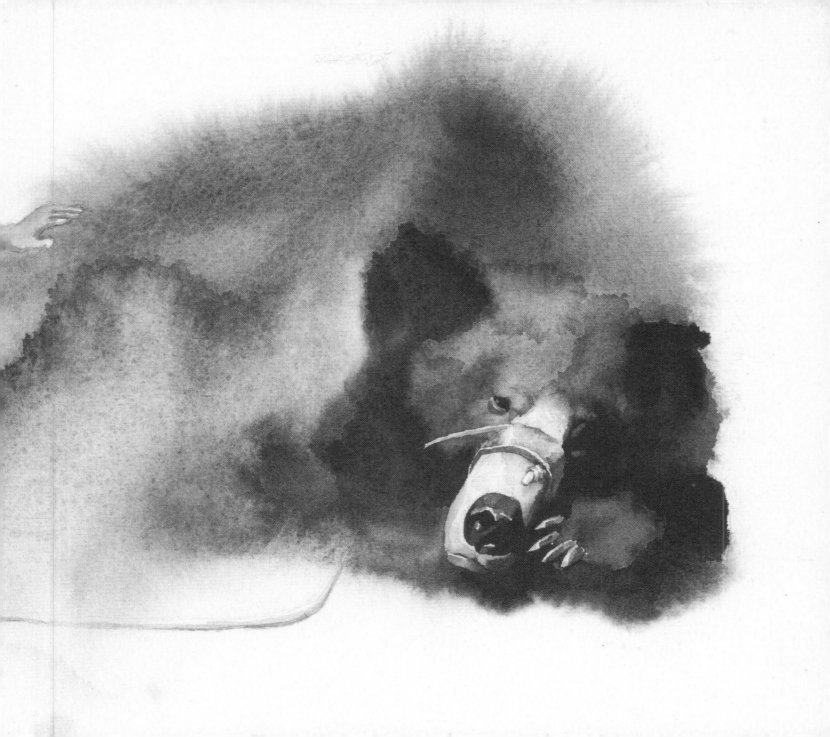

When they reached their street, Altaf could hear people in their courtyard. He quietly snuck in. Bavik Chacha was at the centre, looking angry.

Altaf found his friend Jeeja watching from behind the bushes. 'What happened?' he whispered.

'Bear-rescuers,' said Jeeja grimly. 'They came and took Toufan away. They had a video of Bavik Chacha's show and they've threatened to arrest him.'

'Arrest him?' Altaf was astonished.

'Yes. Bear-dancing is against the law, don't you know?'

Altaf was shocked. 'Who are these bear-rescuers?' he asked.

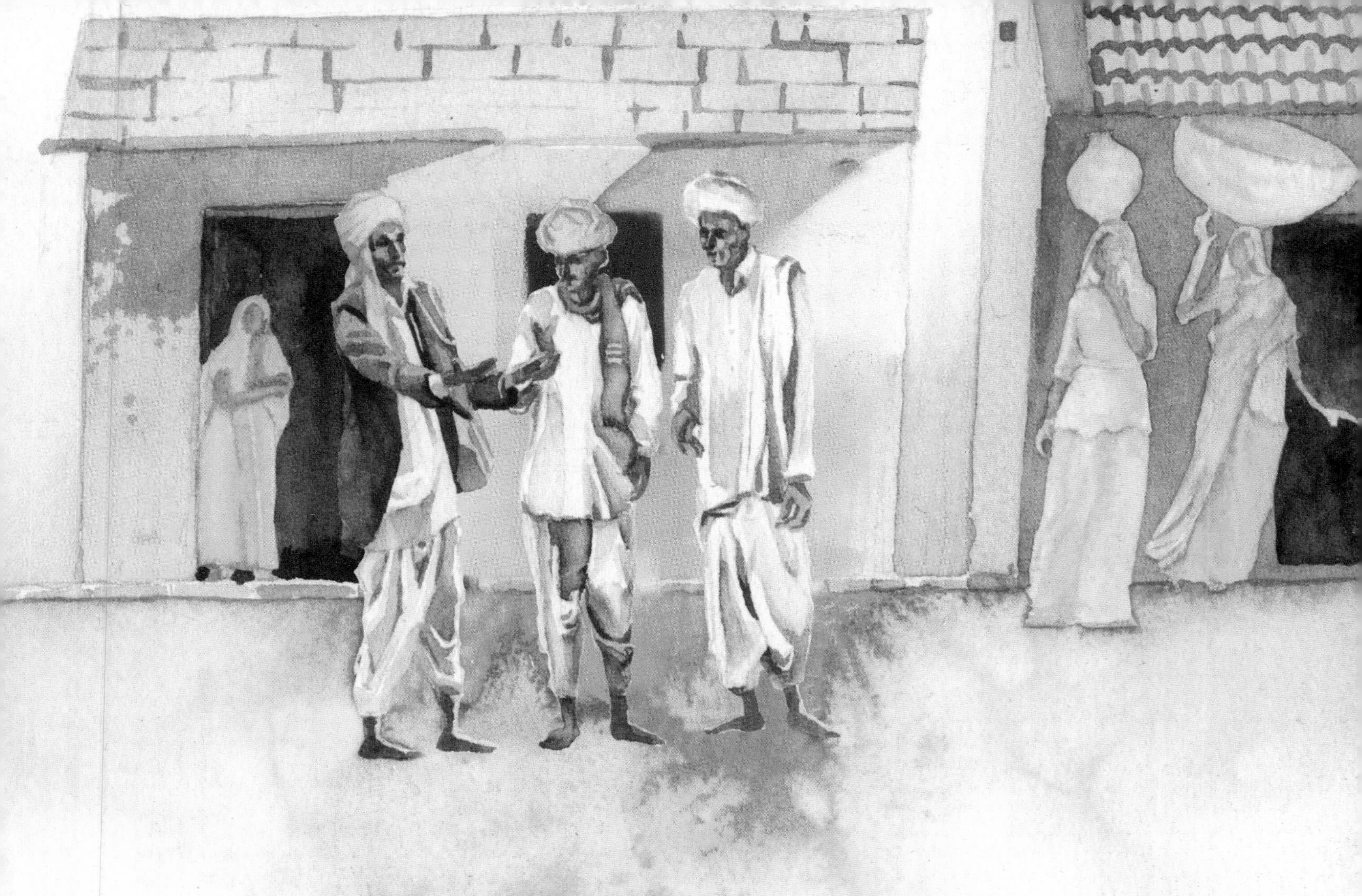

Jeeja shrugged. 'They're from a wildlife reserve. Their office is near the water tank.' Then, Jeeja sharply added, 'Why is Somu still with you? You don't want him taken away too, do you?'

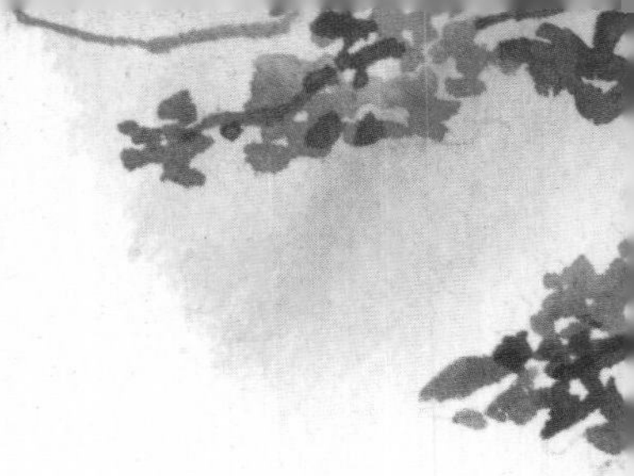

Altaf walked Somu back to the gulmohar tree. He could no longer ignore the feeling in his stomach.

Was he a criminal for making Somu dance? After all, Somu was his friend. And Somu was free, wasn't he?

Altaf looked at Somu, the rope that went through his muzzle, his bleeding mouth and his sad face – no, Somu was neither free nor happy.

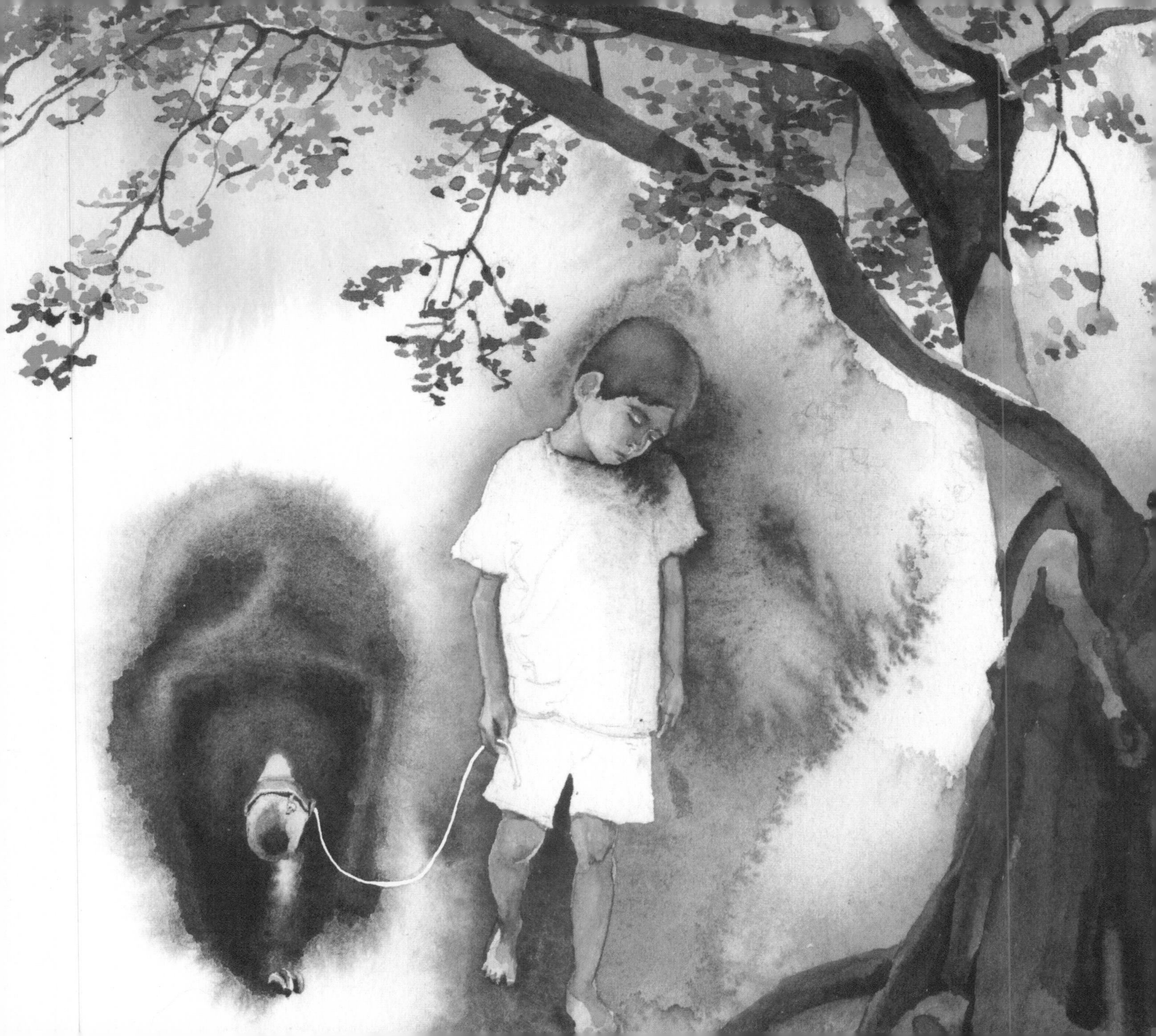

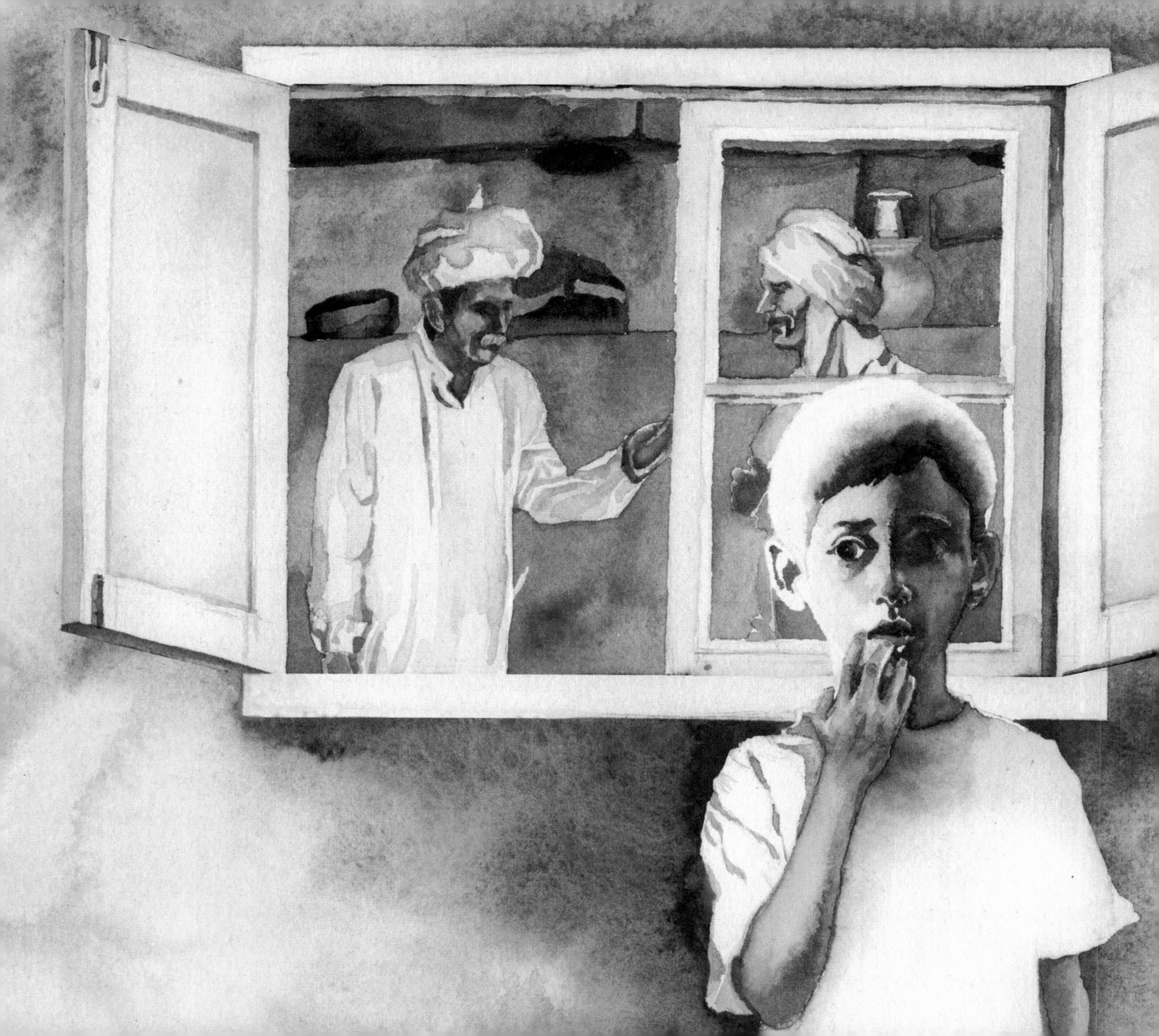

As he walked back, Altaf heard voices from inside the house.

'So is it agreed?' came Bavik Chacha's voice. 'I'll take Somu now that I've lost Toufan?'

'Yes, yes,' Altaf's father replied, 'Altaf will understand. But Somu listens only to Altaf and Jeeja. You'll have to be patient with him.'

Bavik Chacha spoke again. 'Patient? I've worked with bears all my life. I know how to handle them. Somu is a lazy bear. He just needs to be whipped into shape. Nothing a few beatings can't do. And why does Somu still have his teeth? I'll have to remove them myself now.'

'No,' Altaf's father said, 'He's too old now. It will hurt him too much. Let his canines be. He's never bitten anyone.'

'I'm taking no chances,' declared Bavik Chacha, 'I'll pull them out tonight. He'll bleed for a few days, but at least he'll know who's boss.'

Altaf could not believe his ears. How could his father give Somu away? And how could Bavik Chacha talk so openly about beating Somu?

There was only one thing to do now.

That evening, when everyone was busy, Altaf quietly snuck out of the house and headed straight for the water tank.

'Please help me,' Altaf cried when he saw two officers walking out, and simply blurted out the whole story. The bear rescuers listened patiently.

'We're glad you came to us, Altaf,' the woman said. 'Don't worry. We will help you and protect Somu. Now go home. Don't let anyone know that you came here.'

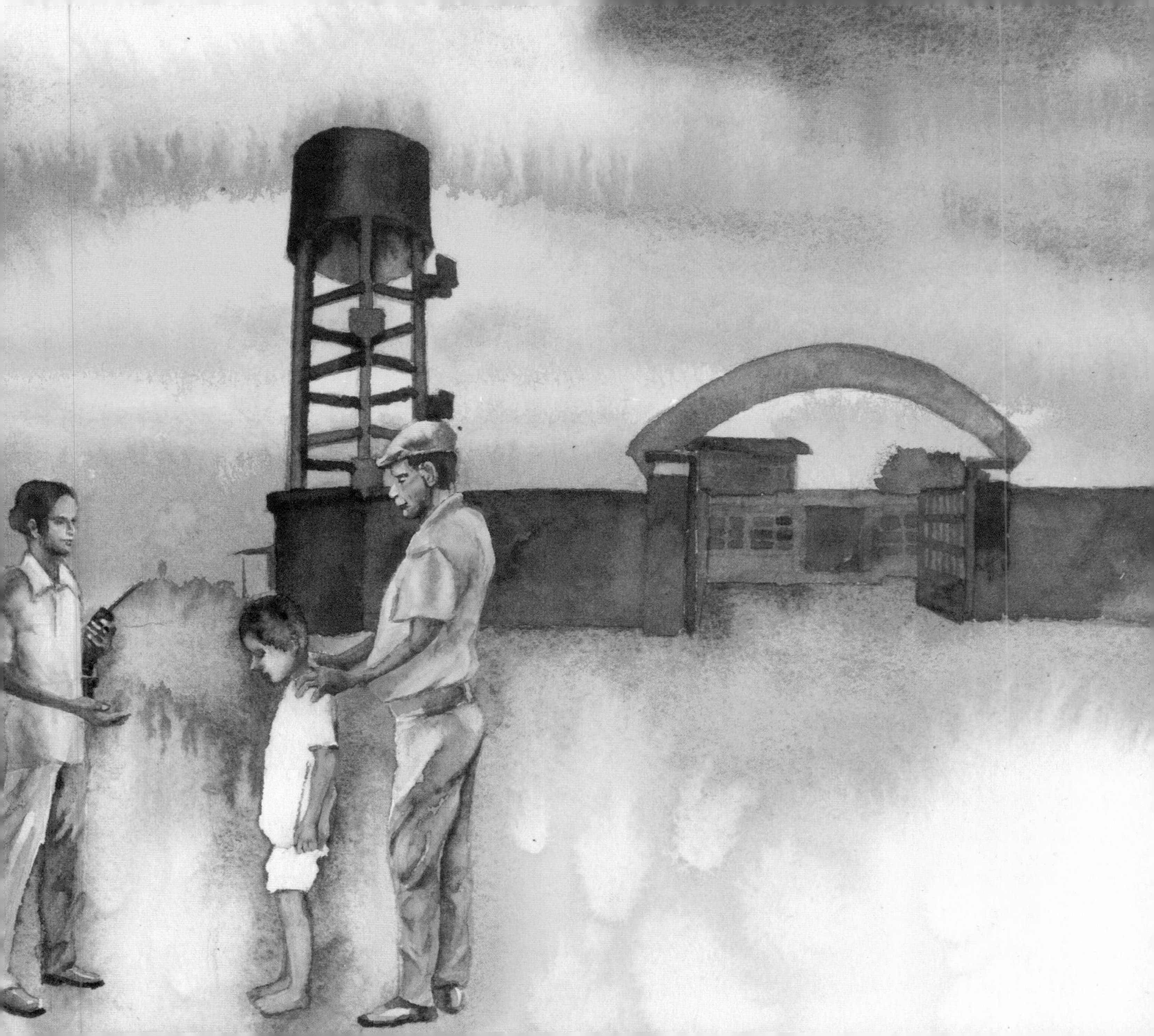

The next morning, a team arrived at Altaf's courtyard again… this time to rescue Somu. As they turned to leave with Somu, Altaf ran to them crying, 'Please take me with you.' Everyone looked shocked. Altaf looked pleadingly at his father, 'Please, Papa?'

Altaf's father looked into Somu's eyes for a moment before shifting his gaze to Altaf. Then, he nodded. 'Take care of Somu,' he said.

Altaf went with Somu to a sanctuary in Agra, where several bears lived. Somu's cuts and bruises were treated and the rope from his muzzle was carefully removed.

'I am so sorry, Somu,' said Altaf, seeing how the rope had left blisters and a large gash around Somu's mouth. The wounds were bandaged and Somu was fed fruits, nuts and warm honey.

Finally, Somu went to sleep. Altaf curled up beside him, also exhausted, but happy.

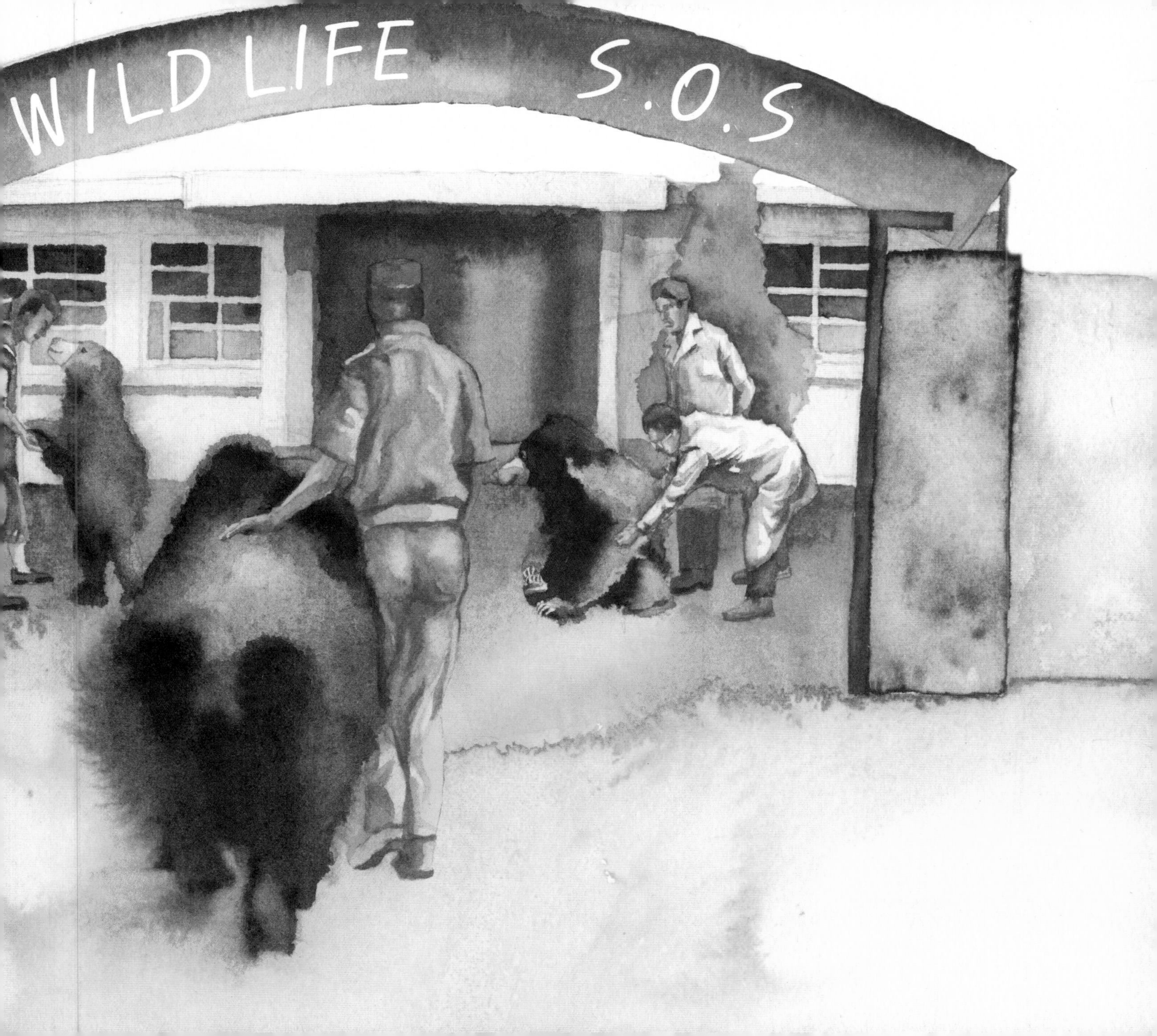
WILDLIFE S.O.S

Altaf did not return home. He stayed back to help at the sanctuary.

The social workers enrolled him at a local school. In his free time, he helped them rescue more bears.

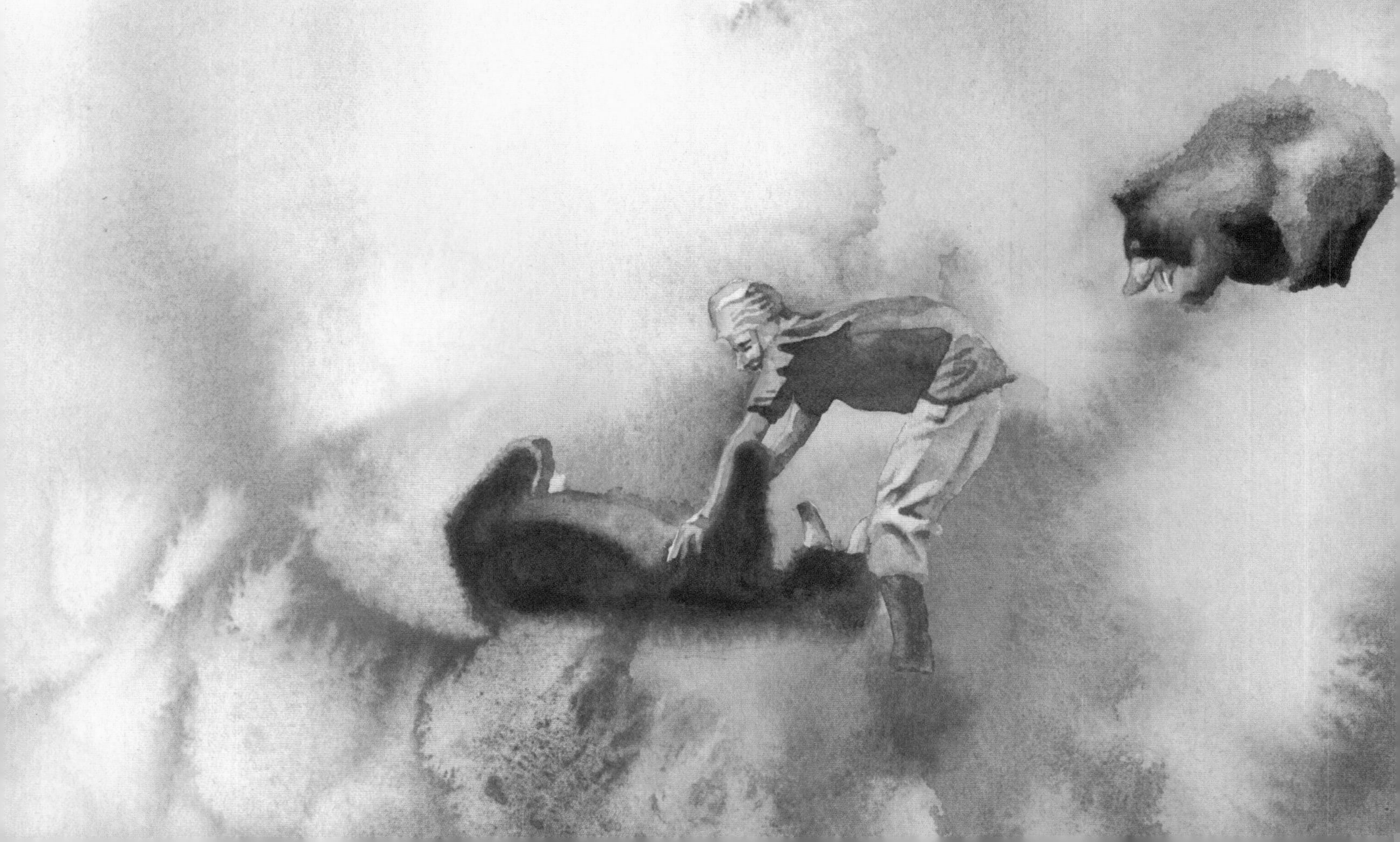

Sometimes, he went back to visit his family and tell them about his work.

Jeeja agreed to bring his bear to the reserve as well. After Jeeja, his father and a few others followed. Bavik Chacha was a little harder to convince.

Altaf loved his job and his school. Best of all, whenever he visited Somu, he saw his old friend's eyes light up and dance with joy.

This was indeed how Altaf wanted his dancing bear!

Dancing Bear

© and ℗ 2011 Karadi Tales Company Pvt. Ltd.

Text: Manasi Subramaniam
Illustrations: Gwangjo, Jung-a Park

Karadi Tales Company Pvt. Ltd.
3A Dev Regency, 11 First Main Road,
Gandhinagar, Adyar,
Chennai 600 020.
Ph: +91 44 4205 4243
Email: contact@karaditales.com
Website: www.karaditales.com

Printed: V & M Prints Pvt. Ltd., Chennai

ISBN No. : 978-81-8190-200-9